I0537547

The Electric Axeman

Ned Fain, Private Investigator,
Book 2

Sam Abbott

Sam Abbott

The Electric Axeman: Ned Fain, Private Investigator,
Book 2
Copyright © 2015 by Liz Dodwell
www.mix-booksonline.com

Print ISBN-10: 1939860245
Print ISBN-13: 978-1-939860-24-8

Published by Mix Books, LLC

This is a work of fiction. Names, characters, places and incidents are the product of the author's imagination or are used fictitiously, and any resemblance to actual persons, living or dead, business, companies, events, or locales is entirely coincidental.

Table of Contents

One

I bought this car a couple weeks ago, when I was working on something that meant I needed to be able to get around the city easily. I hadn't had a car for more than a year, and after that job was over I began to remember why that had been.

It was because I hate the way other people drive.

For some reason, almost everyone on the road seems to think the whole thing was built just for them. They think nothing of cutting someone off, will just about ram you to get in front of you in your lane, and usually don't even have a clue what's going on within ten feet of the two or three tons of metal and glass that they're driving. To me, that's not a good way to stay healthy and in one piece, so I was beginning to think that having the car wasn't necessarily a good idea, after all.

It was a Tuesday morning when I was thinking all this through. I was sitting in the left turn lane at the light on Montgomery Avenue, waiting for the arrow to come on and tell me I could go. The cars on my right were just starting to move, and suddenly, from the corner of my eye, I saw something small come flying through my passenger window. I looked over to see who was throwing crap, and saw a car move out from beside me. A man was driving and a blonde woman was looking past him at me.

Their light was already green and they were moving by the time all this transpired. I cussed myself for having the stupid window down in the first place, and started looking over my shoulder to see if I could cut over and follow the idiots who'd tossed whatever it was into my car!

Sixteen more cars were in the lane beside me, and the one I was wanting to follow was long gone. When my arrow went green, I made my turn and then pulled into a parking space to see what had been thrown at me.

It was one of those little gizmos that you plug into a computer to save things on, a flash drive or thumb drive, I think they're called. I hadn't used one since my time in JAG in the Army, more than a year ago, and didn't really know what they were good for even then. Considering I don't have a computer, it wasn't something I could use, but then again, there could be something of importance on it, something that could lead to its owner. Maybe there would be a reward for returning it; couldn't hurt to try to find out, right?

I glanced around to see if it was safe to pull out onto the street, and noticed a sign in a window beside where I was parked. It said, "Office For Rent, $350."

Now, this is where I should tell you that I had just that very morning gotten my PI license. That's Private Investigator, by the way, not Panty Inspector; yeah, I've heard all the stupid jokes. Anyway, I was still living in the flop hotel I'd been in for more than a year, and I paid more than three fifty a month for that dump. If this place had room for me to live in, as well as make it an office, I could kill two birds with one well-aimed rock.

I shut off the Mustang - yeah, a Mustang, an '08 GT in Vista Blue Metallic, and a monster of a V8 crate motor that someone had sunk a lot of money into before trading it off for a mini-van or something - and got out to check the place over. There was a woman inside, and the door wasn't locked, so I walked in.

The woman - scratch that, she was young enough to call her a girl and not be considered rude -the girl looked up at me as I entered, and I noticed she was something to look at. About five-one, maybe ninety-eight pounds soaking wet, with blonde hair and a pair of the most beautiful brown eyes I've ever seen. She was wearing a light t-shirt and a pair of the most adorable shorts that have ever adorned a derriere, and I smiled my most disarming smile, one that made the scars on my face dance around a bit.

"I see the place is for rent?" I said, and she smiled back.

"Yep. Last tenant skipped out on the landlord, and on me, too. The jerk was my boss, and he still owes me three weeks' pay! I just came to get all my personal stuff, I'll be out of here in a minute. Feel free to look around 'til I leave. I'll yell before I go."

I nodded and looked around for a minute. The place was old, and it wasn't really in the greatest neighborhood, but I didn't see any signs of a leaky roof or mold on the walls. I walked past her to where a door opened into another room. It was also in need of some updated paint and such, but it was like a private office area, and darned if there wasn't a small kitchen on the wall to the left, with a little fridge, a two-burner cookstove and a sink. There was a microwave on the counter, and a coffeemaker, too.

The bathroom was through a door on the other wall, and I peeked in to see that it had a shower, as well as a sink and throne. All in all, I had to say it would be ideal for a new PI who needed to keep costs down.

I went back out to the front office, where the girl was just finishing her packing, and I noticed that she was stuffing a laptop into a case.

"You any good with that?" I asked, and pointed at the little computer.

She glanced at me, and then went on with what she was doing. "I better be, I spent three years in college studying Information Technology. That's what I was doing for the jerk, running his web servers. Unfortunately, he didn't bother to tell me he was a con man, and his websites all disappeared this morning, right along with him and my back pay."

I took the drive gizmo out of the pocket I'd stuck it in. "Can you find out what's on this?"

She looked at it for a moment, then at me. "Are you paying? Like I said, I need money."

"Sure," I said. "It got tossed in my car window a bit ago, and I have no idea what it is or whose it is. If you can tell me, then maybe the owner wants it back bad enough to reward a guy."

She took it and looked it over, then shrugged. "Long as it's not encrypted, no problem." She took the laptop back out of its case and set it on the desk, plugged its power cord into it, then leaned over to plug the other end into the wall outlet. She was bent over away from me, and I heard her say something, but couldn't make out what it was.

"What?" I said. "I'm partly deaf, if I can't see your lips move, I can't make out what you're saying."

She finished what she was doing, then turned to face me. "I asked," she said loudly and slowly, "what's the story behind the scars?"

Why is it people always think that someone with a hearing problem needs them to talk slower? I answered the same way.

"I got blown up by a hand grenade."

She raised her eyebrows. "Guess that explains the hearing, too, right?" She said this perfectly normally, so I figured she got the point of my sarcasm. I lightened up a little.

"Yeah. Took off half my right foot, burned me over sixty percent of my body and left me with half my hearing that's overrun by a constant ringing in my ears."

The laptop was coming on, but I know they take a minute. "I'm Ned Fain, by the way."

"Sylvaine Bouchard," she said, and leaned over to hold a hand out to me. I took it, thought about leaning down to kiss it, but settled for a quick shake instead. "Call me Sylvi, with no 'e' on the end. Everyone does."

The smile she gave me told me that my scars weren't scaring her off, so I smiled a bit wider back. "Nice to meet you."

"Ditto," she said, and then plugged the gizmo into her computer. A little box popped up on the screen, and she sighed. "It's encrypted," she said. "Don't suppose you'd have a guess about the password?"

I stood there for a second, wondering whether to even answer, but she'd been nice, so I was. "Nope. Can you hack into it?"

Sylvi punched a key, and another box popped up. "Probably, but we're looking at a minimum of a few hours of work, here. How much you willing to spend on this project?"

I was still fairly flush from the last job I'd done, with about six grand stashed away in a new bank account, and it occurred to me that I wouldn't mind looking at her for a little while. "How much would you charge me?"

She didn't skip a beat. She looked at me and said, "Fifteen an hour, and that's cheap."

"Deal," I said, "but if I think you're stalling, I'll cut it off."

"Fair enough. You gonna rent this place, or should I take the drive home with me and call you when I get in? If you want to rent it, I can get the landlord down here in five minutes, and by the way, if you offer him three fifty a month, he'll take it. I know, 'cause he offered it to me this morning, but I don't need an office."

I looked around once more. "Call him," I said.

The guy came down from his place up the street five minutes later, and Sylvi introduced us. "Ned, this is Armando. Armando, don't jack with him, he's a friend of mine and I called him down here for you. I told him you'd take the three fifty."

Armando scowled at her for a split second, then shrugged and stuck out a hand to me. "Armando Rodriguez," he said, "and any friend of Sylvi's, y'know? You like this place?"

For less than I was paying each month for a one room flop, I loved it! I took it on a month to month handshake deal, and left Sylvi to work on the gadget while I drove over and cleaned out my old room. Everything I owned fit into a box and a single suitcase, and I was back in less than an hour.

I put my stuff in the private office, and then went to the rent-to-own store about four blocks away to get a couch and chair and a table set. I added in a TV, 'cause I'm hooked on reruns of old shows, and they said they'd deliver it all in an hour. I went back to find Sylvi studying her computer screen.

"Any luck?" I asked, but she shook her head.

"Not yet, but I'm making progress. I know the password only has six digits, but that could be any combination of letters, numbers and special characters, like punctuation. I'm writing a program to try different combinations until it finds the right one."

"Will that take long?"

"There are twenty six possible letters, double that with capitals, and ten numbers, but then we add in the usual thirty two special characters, we've got billions of possible passwords. Computers are fast, but it'll take hours, maybe weeks, to go through that many."

I started calculating some numbers of my own; fifteen bucks an hour times forty hours…

"Relax," she said. "I won't try to soak you for that much time; let's call it a hundred and fifty bucks, total, if it works, okay?"

I agreed, and Sylvi went back to doing whatever she was doing on the computer. When the furniture arrived a bit later, she helped me and the delivery guy get it all in and set up, and then asked me if I was going to hang my license. I hadn't even thought about it, so she scowled, asked me for ten bucks and went to get a picture frame to put it in. Gave me the chance to see her wiggle her way out the door, and I liked it.

When she got back, we worked together to hang it up on the wall. There were plenty of nails already there, but every time I thought I'd found the right place for it, she gave me that scowl and told me to move it somewhere else. When she was finally satisfied, she went back to her computer.

"Ned, this thing's gonna keep working through the night. How about I go on home and come back tomorrow and see how it's doing. Say around nine?"

I nodded agreement. "Yeah, that's fine. You need some money now?"

She hesitated. "I didn't want to ask for an advance…"

"You didn't. I'm offering. I can give you half now, if that'll help."

Sylvi looked down at the floor, and nodded. "Thanks, it really does help. All my bills are overdue, and I don't even have anything to eat at the moment. I kept falling for the boss's BS about how he was just waiting for a check to come in, so he could pay me."

I opened my wallet and pulled out four twenties, as close as I could get to half of a buck fifty, and gave it to her. "Tell you what," I added. "I'm ready for some lunch, myself. I'll buy if you'll fly? Pizza, maybe?"

She looked up at that. "Sure! That sounds great!"

I gave her another twenty, and she headed out the door again. Her car was parked right behind mine, a little Scion sports car, and she made a cute little twist as she got in.

I went to the back room and turned on the TV, which reminded me to call the cable company. Just to get TV would have cost me almost a hundred a month, but then the lady offered me this bundle deal that would give me an office phone and internet along with it, for only another twenty nine a month. When she said the phone had free long distance, I agreed to it just to shut her up! The nice thing was that they could come and install it in only about an hour, so I'd get to watch TV that night.

Sylvi had given me her cell number earlier, so I called her and asked her to grab a cheap office phone, and I'd pay her back for it. She said okay, and I sat there and stared at the walls for a minute, then went out front and sat down at the desk. I looked at her computer. I'd used computers before, you do when you're a lawyer, even in the Army. I hadn't touched one in a year, but everything looked familiar.

I opened her file manager and browsed through it. She had a lot of files that I was sure were for her internet work, but I also ran across a file folder called "Writing," and took a peek inside. It was chock full of stories, poems and the like, and I read a few of them in her word processor. The girl could write, I'll say that for her, and some of the poems were good enough that I thought she ought to publish them.

Of course, then I'd have to admit to snooping, so I closed all of the things I'd opened, and started looking through the desk drawers. Most of them were empty, but I found some legal pads and a box of pens, and a stapler.

Thank God for small favors, I thought, and left them where I'd found them.

Sylvi came in about twenty minutes later with two large supreme pizzas and a cold two liter bottle of root beer. She dug into a cabinet I hadn't even noticed yet and found a couple of plastic cups, poured for both of us and we dug in.

"By the way," she said, "I think you should get the window painted, put your name on it and all. Gotta let people know you're in business, and you might be surprised how many people around here might want a Private Eye."

I looked out the window at the street and neighborhood. "Sylvi, we're in the slums, the red light district, booze joint row."

Her eyebrows went up. That was really cute, and I liked it. "What? You think hookers and winos and drunks don't need help from a private eye once in a while? They're people, aren't they? And believe it or not, most of them have money. I bet you'd even pick up business from women who want their husbands followed. Or vice versa."

I shook my head in resignation. "Don't suppose you know a sign painter, do you?"

She lit up. "Yeah. Moi! And I've got everything I need in the trunk of the car!"

I groaned. "And how much is this gonna cost me?" I asked.

She turned to the computer and opened a program, and I saw that she'd already designed a sign for me.

Ned Fain

Private Investigator

Discreet and Professional

I was surprised, because it actually looked pretty good. She smiled at me and said, "How about I go easy on you? Another sign painter would charge you four hundred bucks, so I'll do it for half of that. Deal?"

A sign like that would be painted onto the inside of the window, in reverse. That meant I could sit here and watch her wiggle her butt all across the window for an hour or two.

"Deal!" I said, and got out the money to hand over. She gave me that dazzling smile of hers again, and wolfed down the rest of her pizza, then went to her car and got her paints and brushes, and a printer for the computer. I watched as she blew the sign up to full size, which meant we could only see one letter at a time, and told it to print. Forty or so sheets of paper later, she started taping it up on the outside, so she could basically trace it on the inside. Pretty smart little girl, she was.

The cable guy showed up while my floor show was in progress, so I had to tear myself away long enough for him to install everything. I shouldn't have worried; the sign took her a good three hours, so I got two and a half hours of delightful ideas that I'd never even think of acting on.

When it was all done, Sylvi and I admired it together for a few minutes, and then she thanked me for the chances to earn some money. "If you hadn't walked in when you did, I'd have been dancing down at the Boom Boom Room by tonight," she said, "and I promised myself when I graduated that I'd never do that again! It paid for my education, but it leaves you feeling slimy, you know?"

What I really knew was that I wished I'd gotten to see her dance, but I just nodded like a wise old man. She packed up her computer and promised to be back in the morning by nine, and I went to my private room to watch some Supernatural reruns. Sam and Dean are sort of heroes to me, because they never let their fears stop them from doing what had to be done.

Someday I wanted to be like them.

Two

I hadn't eaten all of my pizza earlier, so I finished it off for supper with the rest of the root beer. I thought vaguely about going to the liquor store I'd seen two blocks away and grabbing a six pack, but I hadn't had a beer in over two weeks, not since the job that made me want to be a PI, and I was trying to convince myself that I'd quit drinking.

That case I just mentioned was an odd one. Wait, I better back up a bit.

I used to be a lawyer, assigned to the JAG office in Afghanistan, up until a little over a year ago. My gig was prosecuting war criminals, especially those who were supposed to be our allies over there. My last case, one of the Afghan officers I was prosecuting had someone frag me; toss a grenade into the latrine during a break in his trial. I almost didn't survive, but I did. I limp a bit, and more when I've been on my feet too much, and I have scars all over my body from the shrapnel and fire. Lost half of my hearing, too, and the VA hearing aids don't do much more than amplify the noise I can't really understand, anyway.

Anyhow, two weeks or so back, I was in the wrong place at the wrong time and witnessed a murder. Another witness, a girl, was the main suspect, and she tried to hire me as her attorney, but I don't do courtrooms, anymore. Instead, she hired me to investigate the victim's widow, a rich woman who had plenty of motive to get rid of the guy.

The girl swore she was innocent, and I believed her - until she slipped and let out a detail about the murder that only the killer could have known. I had to get a confession on tape, or she would have walked.

That's what made me decide that this was the line of work for me, and since I was already a licensed attorney, getting my PI license was just a formality that only took a few days. That should bring you up to date, so I'll go on with this story.

The place seemed dead without Sylvi around. The place seeming dead reminded me that I was sitting in my new office, which reminded me that I needed to start earning a living again. I thought about how to start making money with my new license, and that led me to thinking of advertising. I called up a guy I knew who worked as an advertising salesman for the biggest newspaper in the city.

"Arnie," I said, "it's Ned Fain. How ya been?"

"Hey, Ned, I'm good. You?"

"I'm sitting here in my new office, and thinking I need to buy you lunch. Game?"

Arnie laughed. "You, buying? This I've got to see! When and where?"

I grinned. Last time we'd had lunch, I'd stuck him with the tab. "Let's do Jake's over on Montrose, and I'm thinking about fifteen minutes. Work for you?"

"It'll work if you're actually bringing money with you. What's the special occasion?"

"I'm not only bringing money to buy lunch with, I'm gonna be spending some on advertising, too. I just got my PI license and I'm opening an office."

There was a low whistle through the phone. "I heard you did some gumshoe work a week or so back, but I thought it was a fluke. You really ready for this? I mean, after what happened, and all?"

Arnie was one of my best friends back in high school. When I'd gotten back from Afghanistan, I was in pretty rough shape; I still had some bandages and silver-screen on the larger burns, and I was walking with a cane as I learned the difference between a whole foot and a half a foot. Arnie'd heard about it, and he'd been one of the first to come and see me after I got settled into my flop.

He asked me to go out for lunch, and I'd been fine until a truck backfired right outside the door of the place. That was when I jumped and ran out the door, leaving Arnie behind with the bill. He laughed it off, but then he got me alone and asked me about how bad the PTSD really was, and I ended up telling him all of it; the grenade, the fire, the feeling that my face was melting off, trying to stand up on a foot that was shredded and had parts of it hanging off in different directions. I told him about the nightmares, the ones that came every night for that first few months, about seeing that grenade bounce off the urinal and land right there at my feet, and waiting for it to go off again and again and again.

Those nightmares were the main reason for my refusal to return to practicing law, because the scene that happened for real was in the latrine at the Administration HQ at Helmand Province. We were holding courts martial in the courtroom on the third floor, and I'd stepped out during a break to use the facilities. I can still remember the sound of the door being pushed open; it's the last thing I ever heard without artificial hearing enhancement.

Ironically, I didn't hear the grenade hit the floor, or at least I don't remember it. Instead, I saw something out of the corner of my eye, and when I looked more closely, I recognized a hand grenade spinning around on the floor beside my foot, and I instinctively began counting down.

One second.

Two seconds.

Three sec…

"I'm ready," I said. "I've got to get over all that someday, right? This way, I'm out in the world again, and making some money, and I don't have to go stand in a courtroom."

I could hear Arnie thinking for a moment, and then he said, "Jake's, it is, fifteen minutes!"

"See you there," I added, and we hung up. I got up and went to the bathroom to clean up a bit, then grabbed my keys and went to the car. Fifteen minutes later, I parked the Mustang in front of Jake's Cafe, a western style place on Montrose Avenue that served some of the best steaks you're ever going to taste in your life!

Arnie was already there, which I kind of expected, since his office is less than two blocks away. I went in and sat down across from him in the booth he'd chosen, and the waitress set a cup of coffee in front of me without even asking me if I wanted it. That was okay, because I did.

"I'm going to warn you now," Arnie said, "I'm ordering a porterhouse. If you run out on me again I'll have to pay for it myself, anyway, so I might as well enjoy it, right? And if you don't, then I'll enjoy it even more because you'll have paid for it."

"Then you're gonna love it," I said to him. "I was serious, Arnie. I need to advertise, get some business started. Let's eat, then you can talk me through how much it'll cost me."

Lunch was good, and the conversation afterward was, too. Arnie set me up with some ads that would get attention, and then called one of his reporter buddies to join us and get him to do a story on me. Playing off my war wounds and how I caught the killer in the case a couple weeks before, the guy came up with an angle that would make me sound like a hero, and still let the article slip out the fact that I was now in business and available for hire. Heck, he made me sound so good, I wanted to hire me!

When we got done, it was almost four in the afternoon, and we finally headed out. I ended up buying lunch for the reporter, too, but the story would come out on the front page of the paper the next week, so it was well worth it. I said goodbye to both of them, and drove back to my office apartment.

I'd been sitting behind the desk for a few minutes, thinking of other ways I might promote myself, when the door opened and a woman walked in. I spent about four seconds thinking those were the very words that most cheap detective novels start out with, then asked, "Can I help you?"

The woman was blonde and very attractive, and it hit me that she looked vaguely familiar. I couldn't quite place her, though, until she said, "I think you have something of mine."

It dawned on me where I'd seen her; she was the woman in the car that passed as the gizmo was tossed into mine. I knew what she was after, but I wasn't ready to admit it.

I grinned my cockiest grin at her. "I've got something you'd want, all right, but I'm not sure we're talking about the same thing. Care to clarify that statement?"

She stood there for a moment, then stuck a hand down into her purse, pulled out a short revolver and pointed it at me. "I want the flash drive that my husband threw into your car yesterday, Mr. Fain, and I don't really care what I have to do to get it back from you. Where is it?"

Sylvi had the gizmo, but I wasn't letting this woman know that. "What fell into my car?"

She moved suddenly, then the gun's barrel was shoved up against my forehead and hurt like the dickens. "Lady, I don't know what it is you want, for crying out loud. If something fell into my car, it must have gone under the seat or something."

The barrel pulled back a couple of inches, and she looked me in the eye. "Then let's go check," she said, "and you'd better hope we find it!"

She backed off a little more, and I slowly turned the chair and got up. I didn't think she really looked the type to pull the trigger, but I wasn't ready to bet my life on it, so I kept my hands in plain sight and walked slowly to the door and through it.

The neighborhood we were in was one that had seen people held at gunpoint before, and while a few people looked at us with curiosity, no one said anything or tried to intervene. Experience had taught them all that doing either one was likely to get them shot, instead of me, so they looked, but said nothing.

I could understand. I was always walking into things I shouldn't, because I don't stop to think before I act. If I did, I probably would have offered to get her the stupid gizmo as soon as she walked in, gotten it out of my life and saved myself a lot of problems. But, no, not me; I've got to be some kind of hero! Solve a mystery, even if all it's doing is costing me money!

We got to the Mustang and it dawned on me that my metallic blue car is probably how she found me. Maybe a PI should drive something more common and mundane, like a plain white Taurus or something. I reached out and opened the passenger door, and the woman tried to shove her head past me to look inside.

For a split second, the gun was pointing away from me, and I spun around and smacked at it, knocking it flying, but then my bad foot twisted a little further than it liked, and the pain shot up my leg and out the top of my head! I reeled, trying to pull the foot back into a normal position, and my messed up ears joined the fray, throwing me completely off balance and dropping me to my knees

Blondie had slapped at me a couple of times, and when she saw me fall, she turned and went for the gun again. It was there in the gutter, and I tried to lunge for it at the same time she did, but I couldn't get any traction with my bad foot, and her hand closed around the grips. She looked at me with something between rage and pure, rapturous glee, and I knew I'd been wrong as she pointed the gun at me. She most definitely was the type to pull the trigger, and all I could hope for was that the caliber was small enough I could survive it.

A foot flashed into my vision, kicking Blondie's hand and sending the gun flying once again. She turned to face her attacker and got a fist across her face that would have rocked most guys bigger than me, and then I saw that her attacker was Sylvi. Blondie tried to recover, but Sylvi was fast as lightning; she did some kind of super-cartwheel, and when she landed back on her feet, that little gun was in her hands and aimed right between Blondie's blue eyes.

The blonde turned and took off running, and a car screeched to a stop in front of her, just long enough for her to get in. It was going down the alley, and I couldn't see the license number as it vanished.

Besides, I wasn't really paying attention to the car; I was staring at Sylvi. She was following Blondie with her eyes, and tracking her with the gun, until the car disappeared down the alleyway. She turned back to me, lowered the gun and passed it to me, grip first.

I finally managed to get to my feet and closed the door on the Mustang. Sylvi looked at me and said, "Bet I can guess what she wanted."

"Three guesses," I said in reply, "and the first two don't count. Let's talk about it inside." I led the way back into the office and we sat down, Sylvi automatically took her old chair behind the desk, and I got the other one, facing it.

"Those were some pretty hot moves," I said. "Do that kinda stuff often?"

She grinned at me. "My dad always said that a girl had to know how to protect herself in this world, so he started me in karate classes when I was six. By the time I was ten, I was junior girls' champ in the region, and I moved on to Mixed Martial Arts classes and loved it, so I kept at it. Still do."

I felt my eyebrows go up about an inch, which is a lot for a guy with scars up there. "I'm impressed. Do you still compete?"

"Nah. I found out it's hard to get a date if all the guys around know you can kick their butt, so I keep it low key, the past couple years." She changed the subject. "She wanted the flash drive, right?"

"Yes, that's what she wanted, and when I couldn't give it to her she apparently was going to kill me, which she didn't get to do thanks to the intervention of Batgirl. Thing is, this means that she's either stupid, or extremely desperate. You don't eliminate the person who has what you want unless you've already gotten it."

"True," Sylvi said. "I've seen enough movies to know that. So, now what?"

I ran that question around my head for a few seconds. "Now, my dear girl with a dragon tattoo, we find out why that thing is so blasted important that it's worth killing over. I want you to keep at it 'til you've got in, tell me everything on it. Tell me how much, and I'll pay you."

She whistled. "Okay. I'll go home and get back on it. You gonna be okay, here? Want to come crash at my place?"

I held up the gun, flipped it open and saw that it was a .32 caliber with six bullets in place. I closed it again and waggled it in the air. "I'm tougher than I look, and now I'm armed, so I'll be okay. Besides, I'm curious to see if she'll come back, or who might show up in her place."

Sylvi looked at me for a long moment, then nodded. "Just be careful," she said. "Ugly as you are, there's something about you that I like, and I hate when my friends get themselves killed. Means going to a funeral, wearing black, all that crap, and it just isn't me."

Before I could come up with a wise-crack comeback, she was up and headed for the door. "Hey," I called out. "Why did you come back in time to save my neck?"

She stopped and looked at me. "Oh!" she said, then ran back over to the desk and reached up under it for a bag that was stashed behind the top drawer, then opened it to show me that it contained tampons. "Emergency stash," she said, and then she was out the door and gone.

Three

The day was pretty well shot, so I rummaged in the fridge and found a couple of burritos and a can of Coke that I'd brought from the flop, heated the Mexican Munchies in the microwave and kicked back with Sam and Dean.

I don't know when I dozed off, but it had to have been around eleven or so. That didn't matter; what did matter was that my clock said it was now three-fifteen, and I'd just been awakened by the light that flashed on the wall in my private room when my front door was opened. Since I knew I'd locked it that meant either someone had picked the lock, or Sylvi was planning to surprise me with something that should only remain in daydreams.

My daydreams don't come true, so I was opting for the lock-picking theory, which meant Blondie or someone on her side of this mess was now sneaking around my front office. I rose as silently as I could, picked up the revolver from my coffee table, and made my way to the door that separated the two rooms. It wasn't completely closed, so I put my eye to the crack and looked.

It was a man, and he was wearing black. He was going through the desk drawers so quietly that I couldn't hear anything at all, even though I had fallen asleep with both hearing aids in place and on high volume. That told me he was a pro, probably a burglar who'd been hired to break in and try to find the gizmo.

I swung the door open quickly and covered the space between me and him in two strides. The cold metal of the gun barrel touched the back of his neck, and he froze.

"Mind tellin' me what you're doing in here in the wee small hours?"

The guy didn't move a muscle. "Looking for something you're not supposed to have. If you just let me have it, all this unpleasant business can go away, and we can both get on with our lives. Deal?"

"Hmm. I've got a better deal. You tell me who you're working for, and I won't pull this trigger. Then we can both get on with our lives."

He laughed. I'm serious; I'm holding a gun to his neck, and he laughs! I couldn't believe it, but I didn't get time to express my disbelief, because he said, "Man, only a fool messes with the Electric Axeman," and then he stood up and ran right out the front door without so much as looking at me.

I couldn't move that fast, so there was no catching him, and I was reluctant to shoot a guy with a gun that I was not licensed to possess, let alone use. I stood there as he vanished, wondering what would make a man less afraid of a loaded gun at his neck than of some comic-book villain with a name like "Electric Axeman?"

I looked outside and he was definitely gone, so I locked the door again. I put a chair against it to keep the next burglar working for a few moments longer, then went back to bed. I stripped off my clothes, tucked the gun under the pillow and lay there watching an infomercial about a blender until I fell asleep again.

The next morning, Sylvi showed up right on time, which meant she got there about half an hour before I would have willingly dragged my carcass out of bed. She still had a key to the door, so she let herself in. Apparently, she didn't have any problems getting past the chair, and next thing I know she's leaning over my bed, barely touching my shoulder and whispering, "Ned - you awake yet?"

"Nope," I said without opening my eyes. "Croaked in my sleep. Put me out with the trash and you can have the rest of my stuff."

"Ha-ha. I brought coffee and doughnuts. Breakfast of PI's everywhere! Get up and put some clothes on, and I might even let you have some." She flaunted herself right back out to the front office. I opened my eyes to watch, and saw that she was wearing a nice little pleated skirt and a sleeveless pink top. Cute.

I looked down over myself and realized that I was in my shorts, and had kicked off the sheets. No wonder she said to get clothes on; she got a full show of my scarecrow routine, scarred chest, legs, mangled foot, everything. I sat up, fumbled on the floor beside the bed and stuffed my feet through the legs of the jeans I'd worn the day before.

Quick couple minutes in the can and I was a new man. I wandered out front and Sylvi handed me a cup of brown liquid that smelled like coffee, and it even had the right amount of sugar in it. "How'd you guess how much sugar?" I asked, and she giggled.

"I watched you yesterday, and the later it got, the less energy you had. Didn't take all of my brains, considerable though they are, to figure out that you start the day with a big sugar rush. So I held up the sugar dispenser over your cup and counted til it felt right."

I thought about that for a moment. "How high did you get to?"

"Nineteen."

"Hmph. Okay." I sat down and reached for a doughnut. Sugar rushes are not made on coffee alone, you know. And they were the cinnamon glazed ones.

Sylvi set up her computer on the desk, and when it came to life she gave a small gasp. "Hey! We got something! We're in!"

I leaned close as she looked through a series of words that seemed to indicate files on the gizmo. She clicked one and it opened up in a spreadsheet. I saw numbers, lots of numbers, and it was easy to tell that some of them were money, 'cause they had dollar signs and decimal points. Some of them were a great big freaking lot of money.

"Any clue what any of that is supposed to mean?" I asked her, but she shrugged.

"I got nuttin', honey," she answered, then pointed at the screen. "See, these green ones are positive numbers, meaning deposits or credits, and the red ones are negative, withdrawals or debits. On the wild side, the yellow numbers are also debits, but they're not showing up anywhere else. I'm thinking this is just one file of a big set, and it looks like you stumbled onto somebody's special set of books, if you know what I mean?"

I knew exactly what she meant. The file we were looking at was part of someone's bookkeeping, and it showed all the income, just as it should, and the expenses - but then there were some other entries that showed money moved from main accounts to somewhere else, and probably in a manner that would not please the IRS or some other alphabet soup group.

Sylvi asked something but I didn't see her lips well enough to catch it. "Again?" I asked, and she turned to face me and said, "I know what these other numbers are," Sylvi smiled. "What do I get if I tell you?"

I thought about a wisecrack, but instead I said, "How about a very nice lunch?"

"Hmm. I guess that'll do, though I was hoping for cash." She leaned close across the desk, like we were conspiring about something. "What you're seeing there is a ledger of Bitcoin transactions. Do you know what Bitcoin is?"

I'd heard of it. "Some kind of funny money on the internet."

"Sort of, yes. It's a digital currency; you buy it with dollars, or euros, or pesos or whatever, and then you can trade it with other people all over the world for things you want. Then, you can sell it right back to a lot of different trading companies for cash again, and it's almost untraceable. Drug dealers are using it, and so are people who just don't think the governments of the world should be able to track how they spend their own money. It's not just for crooks, but a lot of them like it, anyway."

I thought that over. "So this is somebody's business records, and I'm guessing it's a record they'd rather not have floating around, right?"

Sylvi was nodding. "That would be my take, too. I'm betting that your girlfriend, yesterday, wouldn't hesitate to kill you or me or anyone else to get this information back out of sight."

I mulled that around, too. "Then why did her hubby toss it into my car?"

Sylvi winked at me. "Now you're starting to ask the right questions!"

"There's something else," I told her. "Middle of the night, I got a visitor, a cat burglar type. He got in and was going through the desk, looking for you know what. I caught him, even had the gun on him, and it didn't seem to faze him. He told me I was a fool to mess with someone he called 'the Electric Axeman,' and then ignored me and the gun to run off into the night."

Her eyes lit up. "Bingo!" she said. "The username on this ledger is EA, which I bet stands for Electric Axeman. A lot of black market bitcoin traders, especially the bigger ones, use crazy names like that."

I smiled. "Okay, but where does this fit in? If it's just bookkeeping, can it really be traced back to him?"

"That's what I was talking about, these other numbers without dollar signs. Those are account numbers. With all of this info, you could conceivably trace who sent what money to whom, whether it was legal or illegal, and where that money ended up. What I'm seeing here is that someone has funneled about three million dollars from the usual accounts into another one that only shows up one time, here at the end."

It was my turn to let out a low whistle. "Then I can see why they want it back. If this guy is such a bad dude, then he's probably willing to kill if he gets wind that someone has ripped him off." I thought it through for a moment. "So, this Electric Axeman is running some kind of black market deal on the internet, drugs, kiddie porn, something."

"Right."

"He uses bitcoin to make his deals, which is stored in an online account."

"Not quite; it's recorded at an online address, not in an actual account where money is kept, like a bank."

"Okay, an online address. And the gizmo, the flash drive, is how the account is accessed?"

"Right. There's a pass code on it that allows access to that particular account, or address. Without it, it would take even a serious hacker months to get into that account, if ever. And it records all transactions as well, according to the software on it."

I sighed. "Each answer makes more questions. Who tossed it into my car? Why? Who is Blondie, and who was the burglar? And the big question is, do we have any idea whether there was an actual crime involved? For all we know, this Electric Axeman might have moved that money himself, then lost the gizmo. Maybe someone was planning to try to shake him down for it. Wonder if there's a reward?"

She slapped my arm. "Hey! PI! You need to give this to the authorities!"

"Which ones? I mean, without any more info than we've got right now, I don't know who to go to at all, do you?"

We kicked it around for another couple of hours and got nowhere, so we went to Denny's and had lunch there. That got me another hour of her company, which beat just about anything but reruns of Supernatural, but those I can watch on one of a dozen channels, just about any time of the day or night. Sylvi I only got when the fates were smiling on me.

When lunch was over, we went our separate ways again, both of us promising to check in with each other the next day. As long as this mess was going on I thought it wise we each had a backup, and she agreed. I went home and turned on the TV to some of those reruns.

The whole thing kept running through my mind, and I wasn't sure what to do about it. For crying out loud, I didn't even have a client on this case, and I didn't even know if there was a case, at all! I was musing through it for about the ninth time when I suddenly caught something on the TV screen.

It was a picture of Blondie, like a driver's license photo blown up to TV size, but I'd know her anywhere after looking down the barrel of her gun. I paid attention and heard an announcer say that the woman, whose name was Norma Patil, had been found tortured and murdered.

I let that sink in for a few seconds, then picked up my phone and called Sylvi. She answered on the first ring.

"Hey, I've got a couple questions. First, can you make a copy of that gizmo?"

"Yeah, that's easy. Since we have the password, I can just copy it right onto my computer."

"Good girl; do that, and then I need the original. Blondie's been murdered, so this is definitely a police matter, now. Next question: can you track the transactions to their source, find out for me who this Electric Axeman really is?"

She hesitated, and I wondered whether she was thinking over whether she could do it, or whether she wanted to get any further involved. "I think I can, but it'll take some time. Want me to get on it?"

"Yeah. Work overtime, if you need to, I have a feeling I'm gonna want that info as soon as possible."

She agreed, and we got off the phone. I got up and freshened up a bit, then went to pick up the drive from her at her place.

It was the first time I'd been there, and I was surprised; it was a nice little apartment. She opened the door when I knocked, and invited me in, but I was in a hurry.

"Okay," she said, and handed me two identical flash drives. "I figured you'd want a copy, too, and I had a few of these laying around, so I made a duplicate. This one," she said, indicating the one in my left hand, "is the original, and the other is an exact copy."

"Smart girl," I said, and turned to go but she grabbed my arm.

"Ned," she said, "seriously - be careful."

I promised to let her know what happened, and walked away.

I got to the police station twenty minutes later, walked in and told the desk sergeant that I wanted to talk to whoever was handling the murder case on Blondie. They told me to have a seat, and I prayed it wasn't Carlson - a cop I'd met on my first case, a real dork - but I was lucky, or so I thought. A detective named Michael Mulcahy came to get me a few minutes later, and led me to his office.

"Mr. Fain," he said when we were seated, "what can I do for you?"

"I think it's more about what I can do for you," I said, and then launched into the entire story, only leaving out Sylvi's name. He listened and made notes, and when I showed him the drive he took it gingerly, as if it were a bomb. I told him about the burglar and his cryptic comments as well, and then handed over Blondie's little gun.

And then the interrogation began. He wanted to know what my involvement was in this, and I explained again about the gizmo landing in the car at a red light. He wanted to know who was driving the car that it came from, and I said I was pretty sure it was a man, but I couldn't be certain.

"Can you tell me anything about the dead woman?" I asked, and he just looked at me without saying a word for a second, then shot back with, "Why didn't you come forward sooner?"

"With what?" I asked. "Until that woman turned up dead, all I knew was that I had something that somebody wanted, and no idea what any of it meant. You guys would have taken a bored report and blown me off, and you'd probably never have connected the drive to the dead woman."

He scowled at me, and I scowled right back. That's what I got for trying to do my civic duty. I got up and left in disgust.

When I got back to my place I didn't stop to check before walking in, and suddenly I was grabbed and slammed against the wall. A voice asked, "Where's the flash drive, friend?"

I recognized the voice of the burglar from the night before. "I just got back from giving it to the cops," I said. "I couldn't crack it, so I thought maybe they could."

"Fat chance of that," he mumbled, and I realized that he wasn't the one holding me. A second later I felt something whack me across the back of my head, and decided it was a good time to play possum. I slumped into the guy holding me against the wall, and he dragged me to a chair and dropped me on it, then began tying me up with rope they'd apparently brought along. I continued to pretend to be out cold.

The burglar picked up my keys from where I'd dropped them when I'd been grabbed, and told the other guy to go search the car. "But not here; take it around the back into the alley."

I heard the door open and close, and then a big cup of water was thrown into my face. I sputtered instinctively, and pretended to be waking up.

"Where is Vijay Patil?" he asked me, and I shook my head.

"Who? I don't know who that is." Patil had been the dead woman's name, I remembered, so Vijay must be her husband, the one she said threw the gizmo into my car. I figured that out instantly, but tried not to let any sign of it show on my face.

The punch came from nowhere, and rocked my head so hard I thought it was going to fall off.

"Where is Vijay Patil?" he asked again. I spat out a mouthful of blood, and said, "I told you, I don't know the guy!" At the same time it hit me that Patil must still be alive, and probably in hiding for his life. Smart man!

I braced myself for another blow and I wasn't disappointed. Another mouthful of blood hit the floor, and one of my back molars went with it.

"Where is Mr. Patil?" Burglar asked, and I shook my head as if to clear it. I was about to say once more that I didn't know, when the other guy came back in.

"Nothin' in the car," he said. "Want me to help? It's amazing what a broken finger or two can do to loosen a tongue."

Burglar nodded, and the guy moved toward me. He reached out and took hold of my right hand, and that's when the door opened again.

I tried to look past the men, praying that it wasn't Sylvi coming in to check on me, but I lucked out. The woman standing just inside was about sixty, and as I watched, she went from a polite smile to a full blown, air raid siren scream that almost took off the top of my head. She stumbled backwards out the door again, still screaming at the top of her lungs.

The two guys looked at me and then at each other. Burglar said, "We'll be back," and the two of them hot-footed it out the door like scared kids. I saw them shove the screaming woman down onto her backside, and then they were gone.

Somebody called 911, and a few minutes later I had EMT's and Detective Mulcahy in my face. The medics wanted to take me to the hospital, but nothing was broken except that one tooth, and I refused. So they fussed over the screaming woman, instead. Turns out she was soliciting donations for the local soup kitchen. Meanwhile I filled Mulcahy in on what had happened. He listened and took his notes, then looked at me.

"Patil is the husband of the woman we found dead," he said, "and he hasn't been seen since. This indicates he might still be alive." He closed his notebook. "The Electric Axeman is a big time drug lord, and we've been after him for years. He's a ghost; no one knows who he actually is, what he looks like, nothing, and any of his people we get our hands on tend to take whatever we throw at them and keep quiet. That is, if they even live to go to trial. Quite a few of them die of drug overdoses before then. You've got yourself in over your head on this, Fain. I'd suggest you get out of it. Leave it to us."

I stared at him and I'm sure the look of disgust on my face was crystal clear. "I was out of it," I said. "That's why I gave the thing to you, remember? Doesn't look like you're doing too well with it, though, does it?"

He shrugged his shoulders and walked out without another word, and I went to my room to try to rest and get my head on straight. First, though, I thought I should call Sylvi and warn her. If those goons had been watching me this morning, they might know about her, and I wanted her to go into hiding, fast.

It's always a bad thing when a single girl's phone is answered by a man, but it's doubly bad when his first words are, "Hello, Mr. Fain. I am the Electric Axeman. I believe you and I need to make a trade."

Four

"A trade is a possibility," I said, "as long as the girl is alive and safe."

There was a deep laugh through the phone. "She is alive; safe, now? That depends on you, Mr. Fain."

The phone was moved, and Sylvi's voice came on. "I'm okay, Ned. You gonna get me out of this?"

"Or die trying," I said, and then the other voice returned.

"Here are the terms of the transaction. There is a large parking lot at the old appliance factory outside of town; do you know the place?"

"I do."

"In two hours, you will drive there, alone. There is an abandoned Fiat sitting off to the south side of the lot. Put my device on its dashboard, and then drive away. Return in twenty minutes; if I am satisfied, the girl will be in the car, unharmed. She has been blindfolded and has not seen my face, so I have no aversion to letting her live."

"Okay," I said, "but let me add something. If she is harmed in any way, Mr. Axeman, I will hunt you down and I will skin you alive. It will take me many days to do it, and I will not let you die until I am finished. Do I make myself clear?"

He laughed again. "Perfectly, Mr. Fain. You and I both understand the value of violence in this world. I think we can come to a successful conclusion to this transaction. Good bye for now."

The phone went dead in my hand, and I thought fast and hard. I didn't trust him not to kill Sylvi, no matter what he'd said, so I needed to find a way to get to him before he could do that. The cops had been trying to identify this guy for years; I had less than two hours.

I used my phone's Google search to find out where the Patils had lived. It was in Meadow View, a new condo complex that had been built while I was in the Middle East. I hurried out the door to find my car, and it was still in the alley.

It was trashed, even the leather seats ripped up, and the stereo had been torn out of the dash. I promised myself that I would make someone pay for the damage as I fired it up and slammed it into gear. Black streaks followed all the way down the alley, and I left more on the street as I roared around the corner.

I got to Meadow View, and spotted the right unit as soon as I got onto their floor, the crime scene tape giving it away. There were no cops around, so I used an old debit card to slip the lock and was inside.

This place had also been ransacked, everything thrown around like wild bears had been hunting for Goldilocks! There was an office but everything was gone, and like my seats, all the furniture was torn to shreds. I looked for any clue to where Patil might be hiding, but found nothing.

My phone rang; it was Sylvi's cell number, and I answered. "Yeah?"

The Axeman's voice came on again. "I thought you'd need a little extra motivation, Mr. Fain. Please listen closely."

I could hear the phone being held out, and then I heard a scream. I didn't need anyone to tell me it was Sylvi; even in agony I could recognize her voice.

The Axeman came back on. "She is not harmed, Mr. Fain, but I am always amazed at how much pain the brain perceives from a simple, severe pinching on the fleshy part of the back of the arm. The scream is identical to one of genuine agony, don't you agree?"

"You son of a..."

The line was dead, so I didn't bother finishing that sentiment. I was in a rage, and needed to cool my head, so I went into the bathroom to splash water into my face. I reached out to the faucet on the sink, and it hit me that the bottom of the sink was already wet.

I looked at it, wondering how that could be, when the faucet wasn't dripping. I looked around and saw a towel hanging beside me, touched it, and found it damp. Someone had used this sink to wash his face not long ago, and the only one I could imagine doing so was Patil. He was somewhere nearby, sneaking in to get clothes and such. It had to be somewhere that didn't have running water, so he wasn't hiding with a neighbor; and yet, I was sure he was in this building somewhere!

I left the condo and saw a woman coming out of the elevator. I smiled the best I could with scars and bruises.

"Hi, Ma'am," I said. "I'm an insurance appraiser, and I was asked to come and look over the building. Can you tell me if there are storage units for the condo owners?"

The lady was obviously a little taken aback by my appearance, but she tried to smile anyway.

"Well, y-yes," she stammered. "They cost extra on the monthly fees, you know, but they're in the last building, back in the back, in the basement."

"Thank you, Ma'am," I said, and headed in the direction she'd indicated.

There were about three dozen units in that basement, and I was surprised at how easily I got into it; all it took was one good slap on the door, and it popped open. Each unit was marked with a name, except one, which showed signs of having a name tag recently ripped off of it. I was sure I'd found my guy.

There was no lock on it, so I opened the door and stepped inside. Patil was there, lying on a mattress on the floor of the unit, sound asleep. I shut the door behind me, quietly, and nudged him with my bad foot.

He sat up instantly, a look of sheer terror in his eyes. "Shh," I said, putting a finger to my lips. "I'm not here to hurt you. I'm a private investigator, and I'm trying to find the guy who's looking for you."

Patil sat there for a long moment, then began to cry. "I am sorry," he said, "but I am so frightened. I don't know what to do."

I nodded consolingly. "I know, man, I know. Start out by telling me what is so important about that flash drive you threw in my car that people are being killed over it."

He sobbed for a moment, and I'm sure he was thinking of his wife. "It... my wife, she likes nice things - nice, expensive things, and we were getting further and further in debt. I begged her to stop spending but she said everything would be OK if I took the money from my employer, and I could not refuse her. I thought that I could do it and he would not know, you see. But I was wrong. He called me and said that there was something wrong with his accounts, that there was a large sum of money missing, and he wanted me to find out where it had gone." He took a deep breath, and steadied himself.

"I told Norma that I had to put the money back, that if we tried to keep it, he would find out it was me and we would be killed, but she insisted that I could not do that. We were fighting about it, over and over, and finally I threw the thumb drive out the window as we drove. I didn't look where I threw it, I just wanted rid of it so I could go and put the money back, and no one would be knowing what I had done. She saw it go into your car, and no matter what I said, she would not let it go, and then she told me she had found you and we could go and take it back, but I did not want to. She made me take her, though, and she tried to get it from you, but she said another woman fought her, and when I saw her running away from you, I drove and got her and we fled."

He stopped there, and I let him rest a moment. "How did they find out about her?" I asked softly.

Once again, he took a deep breath, and then he said, "Someone else was looking at the records, and they saw that I had transferred three million dollars to a new account I had set up. Somehow, that account was traced to me, and they came to get me, but she was at home alone." He sobbed again, a deep, wracking sob that even I could feel. "They cut off her breasts. They cut off her lips. I do not know what she told them, but they are now looking for me and I didn't know where else to hide."

"Can you tell me who your employer is?"

Patil nodded. "Yes. His name is Eric Spellman. He calls himself the Electric Axeman."

I patted his shoulder. "Good. Now, would you have an address for Spellman?"

He nodded again. "Yes. He lives at 19525 Cherry Hill Lane, Apartment 500."

It was a ritzy neighborhood, with big, fancy condos and offices in each building. Lots of people lived and worked under the same roof, down there. Guy must be worth some serious money to live there. I'd heard that a condo in that complex was more than a million dollars.

"Okay, here's what you do. You stay here for now, and I'll try to make sure this all comes to an end. I can't do anything about your wife, but I'm going to try to get you your life back. Okay?"

He nodded once again, and I slipped out the way I'd come in. I hurried to my car and headed for Cherry Hill

Lane. I was almost there when two patrol cars and an unmarked came barreling around the corner from the other direction, sliding to a stop in front of the building. I parked close and jumped out to run right into Mulcahy.

"What are you doing here, Fain?" Mulcahy asked me.

"I traced the Electric Axeman here, and he's got a girl hostage who's a friend of mine. I want in."

"No way!" he said. "We've got him, and it's mostly thanks to you, but it's time to let real cops do what needs to be done."

I stared at him. "Listen, as soon as he knows you're here, my friend is probably dead! I'm not sitting it out..."

"You will," he said, shoving a finger into my chest, "or you'll sit in cuffs in the back of my car 'til it's over! Got that? Now get your butt out of my way, and stand clear!"

He turned toward the front of the building as two more patrol units pulled up, and forgot me in a split second. I ran around the side of the building while he was distracted and spotted a service entrance.

I tried the door, but it needed a code to open it. There was a small glass window in it, and I started looking for a rock, something I could use to break it in.

Suddenly the door opened, and a Hispanic fellow came running out and disappeared toward the back of the building. I caught the door with my bad foot a split second before it would have closed again. The automatic closer was very strong, and I could feel one of the remaining bones in that foot snap, but I'd lived with foot pain for a year now. I snatched the door open and ran inside, moving as fast as I could on a doubly-injured hoofer.

I didn't think taking the elevator would be a good idea, so I made my way up the steps, all five flights, and my foot was screaming like a banshee by the time I got to the fifth floor. I peeked out and saw that number five hundred was directly opposite where I stood.

I opened the fire door that separated the stairs from the hallway and stepped out. There was no one in sight, but, even though I couldn't make out what they were saying, I could hear voices through the door of the apartment. I stood outside, out of sight of the peephole, and wondered for a moment what to do.

I heard a scream then, and stopped thinking; like I said before, I don't always think before I act, and the scream had been Sylvi. I hit the door with everything I had, and while it may have been an expensive place to live, it had some crappy, cheap doors. It splintered and I fell through, barely catching myself before I sprawled out on my face.

I took in the scene in a split second: Sylvi was on her feet, her hands bound, between two men, both of whom were holding guns. One of them pointed his gun at me and fired, but as he pulled the trigger, Sylvi brought her left knee up and caught him in the gut. His shot nicked me on my right shoulder, but I was already moving, lunging, and I drove my head right into the same spot Sylvi had just kneed. He went down with a woof, and I landed on top of him.

I reached for his gun, but it skittered away, and I turned to look at Sylvi. She was not blindfolded, so I knew the Axeman had been lying about her not seeing his face. The goon under me was out cold, or close enough, but the other guy had his gun pointed at Sylvi's head.

"Mr. Fain," he said, and I knew the voice was the Axeman. I was shocked, because I'd made him up in my mind to be some monstrous creature, huge and strong. He wasn't, though, except for his gun. Eric Spellman was a little guy, about five-four, and he looked about as tough as a chihuahua puppy.

Of course, there was that gun. He smiled at me and said, "I'm afraid you have not held up your end of the transaction, Mr. Fain, and so I am under no obligation to hold up my own. Say goodbye to Miss Bouchard, please." He pressed the gun against her temple and I could see him slowly squeezing the trigger.

"Spellman, the place is surrounded by cops," I shouted at him. "You can't get out. If you kill her, they'll only add more to your sentence. Let her go, man, just let her go!"

He looked at me, and laughed again. "Do you think, Mr. Fain, that they can inject me lethally more than once? But you are wrong, again, as always, because I most certainly can escape. You see, Mr. Fain, Eric Spellman is only a name I created; he does not exist, and no one knows what I look like, save the few that I trust completely, and now the two of you, who are about to be dead anyway."

He turned his attention back to Sylvi, and I was torn; if I moved, he would squeeze that trigger instantly, and if I didn't, he would do it anyway, a second later. I prepared to launch myself at him, thinking that the best I could do was try to avenge her death, when she suddenly whipped both of her feet upward.

The gun went off, but her head had dropped just below the muzzle, and the bullet merely ripped out some hair. When she hit the floor, she snapped both legs out, curled them around Spellman's ankles, and rolled, bring him crashing toward me.

He was caught so off guard that he threw the gun away while trying to get his hands out to catch himself, and I threw myself forward so that I caught him by the throat as he hit the floor. We rolled over once so that I ended up on top of him, and the rage that took me was one I'd never felt before. I struck him across his face, the same way his goon had struck me, and when the blood sprayed out all over the both of us I felt vindicated!

He tried once or twice to block me, but it didn't work. His hands were not strong enough to resist my anger, and I must have hit him a dozen times before I realized the words that were coming out of my mouth.

"I—SAID—DO—NOT—HARM—A—HAIR—ON—HER—HEAD!" I was chanting it, over and over, like a mantra, and suddenly I realized that Sylvi was standing beside me, holding the gun that had only moments before been aimed at her head. She had it pointed at the Axeman, but her finger was outside the trigger guard, so I knew she was not intending to shoot him unless she had to.

"I think he gets the point, Ned," she said, and that's when it dawned on me that Spellman was either unconscious or dead. At that moment, I didn't care which one, but when Mulcahy and a half dozen uniforms burst in a moment later, I was relieved to see that he was still breathing.

Mulcahy was enraged at seeing me there, but when Sylvi got done ripping him a new one, he swallowed his pride and told me I'd done a good job. She'd pointed out that without my intervention, she would be dead, and that got me out of too much hot water for "interfering with a police operation."

Five

Sylvi and I spent the next several hours downtown, giving statement after statement. Spellman had been arrested, and thanks to the information I'd given the police with the gizmo, they'd been able to connect him to most of the biggest drug operations in our part of the country, as well as more than two dozen murders that he had either committed or orchestrated, including that of Norma Patil.

I told Mulcahy where to find Vijay Patil, and they brought him in to make a positive identification of Spellman as the Electric Axeman. A prosecutor came in and promised Patil immunity in return for his testimony, and the little fellow agreed. It was all he could do for his late wife, he said, to see her killer sent to the death chamber.

That same prosecutor came to see me, as well, around ten o'clock that night. I was still in the interrogation room, and he walked in and held out a hand, so I shook it.

"Mr. Fain," he said, then opened up a file as he sat down across from me at the table. "Mr. Fain. The United States government has been after the person known as the Electric Axeman for almost six years, but until today, there was never any way to identify him. He has been the most elusive criminal in almost all of American history, and because of this, a special unit of the DEA was set up to try to track and identify this person, but to no avail. Last year, in an effort to get someone in his organization to step forward, the Government Accounting Office, in cooperation with the DEA, the FBI and the Justice Department, authorized a reward of two hundred and fifty thousand dollars for information leading to his identification and arrest."

I think my jaw dropped to my knees. "Two hundred and fifty grand?" I said, incredulously.

He smiled. "That's what I said. And because the information you provided, as well as your own involvement in the final moments of the case, helped bring about his capture, I received a call a couple of hours ago instructing me to release fifty thousand dollars of those funds to you." OK, it wasn't the full two fifty but to a starving PI it was a fortune.

"The way this works," the prosecutor went on, "is, you get half of it now," and he slid a check out of the file to me, "and the rest when he is convicted and sentenced. Congratulations, Mr. Fain, and may I express the appreciation of a grateful nation."

He shook my hand again, and walked out. A moment later, Mulcahy walked in and looked at me. "We're all done, Fain. And after all that I've heard tonight, I've got to say, you did good for an ex-lawyer turned PI. But can I give you some advice?"

Numbly, I nodded. "Sure."

"Take some of that money and buy a gun, then get a permit to carry it. I've got a strong feeling you're gonna need it now and then." He turned and was gone, and I sat there a minute more before I tucked the check into a pocket and left the room.

Sylvi was waiting for me out in the hallway and got up when I came out. "What was that all about?" she asked, and I almost told her, but something told me to keep my mouth shut about the money.

"They're saying I did a good deed, bringing them the gizmo; that it was the thing that led them to Spellman."

She smiled. "My hero," she said in a cute little voice, tucking her hands under her chin. Then she got serious. "You really are, you know. When they grabbed me, and called you, somehow I knew that you'd come and get me. If you hadn't shown up when you did they were going to kill me and throw my body out the window as a diversion of some kind, to help them get away. When you distracted the one guy, I got a chance to fight, and then when he was down I took the chance of trying to get under the gun and dropping the Axeman. I knew you'd handle the rest."

She said that last with that beautiful smile of hers beaming at me.

I tried not to blush, and the good thing about scars is that they don't let it show. I did my best John Wayne. "Aw, shucks, little lady, 'tweren't nothin' at all! And besides," I went on in my own voice, "I owed you one, remember? You saved me from the crazy blonde lady, so it was sort of an obligation."

"Bull. When I asked you if you were going to come and get me out of there, you said you'd do it or die trying, and I knew, I knew right then, that you were being completely honest. You would have died with me rather than leave me there to die alone."

I looked away from her. "Yeah, well, I don't always think before I open my big mouth..."

That was as far as I got before she grabbed my hair and pulled me down for a kiss. It wasn't a passionate kiss, or a sexual kiss - it was a kiss, that's all, and I almost fainted from surprise. When she let me go, I stood there for a second, still puckered, and she giggled at me.

"Come on, PI," she said. "Let's get you home and into a nice hot shower so you can get some sleep."

I wasn't about to argue. We left the station and got into my car, Sylvi giving it a look that said she was as mad about the damage as I was. I chuckled as I realized that, with the big reward I'd just gotten for helping to nab the Axeman, you could say that he was actually going to pay for the repairs. That made me happy.

I had liked the idea of her getting me into the shower, but she had been speaking figuratively, apparently, because I dropped her off at her place before heading for home. She leaned over and gave me another little kiss on my cheek, and promised to call me in the morning. I smiled and drove off.

I'd gone about a half mile when I saw them: the Burglar and his pal, standing in the parking lot of a convenience store. As usual, I didn't think, and whipped the Mustang around in a bootlegger one eighty that would have made Bo and Luke Duke proud, then roared into the lot straight at them. They saw me at the same time and dived out of the way, then raced toward a late model Corvette and went over the doors to get in. I heard it fire up and they were laying rubber out onto the street.

I spun the wheel and floored it, and the big engine that someone had spent a fortune installing in my car spun me around like it was cracking a whip. I was on them before they'd gone a hundred yards, and I stayed on them as their stock Corvette flew down the streets at more than a hundred miles an hour. I took every corner they did, took every curve and flew over every hump in the road, but they couldn't lose me.

Finally they took off out Old Route 27, and I stayed on their tails. The road was straight, and my digital speedometer was showing me some unbelievable numbers. We passed a hundred and thirty five, and that seemed to be all the Corvette could do, but I could still feel pedal under my mangled foot, so I goosed it and tapped the back of their car.

The Burglar was in the passenger seat, and I saw him raise himself up and turn toward me, an automatic in his hand. I punched the accelerator again, and this time I hit them with enough force to crack the fiberglass on their rear end. The Corvette skidded sideways, and the Burglar lost his grip and tumbled out over the passenger door. The back wheel on that side rolled over his chest, the whole car jumping as the rear end was thrown into the air for a second.

I swerved just enough to miss running him over myself, but I doubted he would survive. I stayed on the Corvette, following the driver and staying no more than five feet from his tail end. If he'd hit his brakes we'd both have died at those speeds, but I was in a mood I'd never experienced before. He wasn't getting away from me.

We were several miles out of town and there was no traffic. I was getting tired of our cat and mouse game, but I didn't know how to make the goon stop, and he wasn't having any luck losing me. I tapped him again and he started swerving all over the road, so I backed off to see what was happening.

A second later big chunks of his left back tire came flying at me, bouncing off my hood and windshield, and then I heard it blow out. We were still doing about one thirty, and the Corvette went into a sideways skid that left no hope for recovery. I slammed on my brakes, slowing almost imperceptibly at first, but then the gap between us began to grow just as the car began to flip over and over and over.

I counted twenty six rolls before it came to rest on its top. The driver had belted in, I could tell, because every time it rolled, I could see him - or what was left of him. By the time it stopped, there wasn't much.

I pulled up close to the wreckage and put the car in park. The Corvette was on fire in spots, but I got out anyway and walked over to look at it. I was right; there wasn't much left of the driver, or of the Corvette, for that matter. I don't think there were more than a few pieces of fiberglass left on it, and only one of the wheels still had a tire.

I turned back and got into the Mustang, then turned it around and headed back to where the Burglar's body had fallen. I found the spot easily enough, by the blood stains; but he was gone. It was possible he'd been dragged off by an animal, I guessed, but I suspected he might have actually survived and was hiding in the brush around the area. That made me feel vulnerable, so I drove on.

If what I had just done were to be known by the police, I could conceivably be charged with vehicular manslaughter, possibly even murder. I'd never seen combat when I was in the army, and the only dead bodies I'd seen were in photographs. And yet, the knowledge that I had just caused the deaths of at least one, and possibly two men, didn't faze me in the least.

I stopped at a gas station that was closed and got out to inspect the car under the lights but didn't see any visible damage. The front bumper had made the only impacts, and since my car and the Corvette had been almost the same color there weren't any real paint scuffs to show. I'd need to buff it out, but I could probably claim the damage had occurred while it was being ransacked.

I drove on home, and parked it on the street, then went inside. I hurt everywhere, and my foot was threatening to demand I cut it off, but I ignored it and went to get into that hot shower. Ten minutes later I was moaning with relief as a lot of the soreness seemed to rinse away. I stood there until the water started to cool off, then walked out into my room to find a pair of shorts, fell onto the couch and grabbed the TV remote.

I don't think I ever got it turned on before I was asleep.

Or maybe Sylvi turned it off. I woke to find her leaning over me again, whispering, "Ned? You awake?"

I opened one eye and looked at her, because the other one was buried in my pillow. "I am now," I said. And you better have coffee."

She smiled that dazzling smile and held a large cup before my eye. I forced myself up to a sitting position and took it, and didn't even worry about her seeing my scars or foot, because she flopped down beside me with her own cup and a bag of doughnuts. She opened the bag and handed me a cinnamon glazed.

"So," she said, "I was thinking. You, my dear PI, need a secretary who is also a computer whiz and has a black belt in several different disciplines, and I know just the girl!"

"You do? Is she cute?"

She shrugged. "She's not bad, but you can't have everything. And she also knows how you like your coffee, and what kind of doughnuts you like best. Those are perks, right?"

"Could be. How is she at housekeeping and washing dishes?"

"Hey!" she said sternly. "She's not that kind of girl! Although, for a few extra dollars you can probably get her to tidy up around here once in a while. You haven't been here a week yet, and this place looks like my kid brother's room!"

I looked around. Okay, so some of my dirty clothes were laying on the floor here and there, and the odd empty pizza box and two-liter was laying about, but it wasn't all that bad, I didn't think.

"We haven't even discussed her pay yet, and you've got her asking for a bonus? She better be more than cute!"

"Oh, she really is quite the little doll, to be honest. And while she won't do anything immoral, well, other than the occasional hacking job, she might not object to being taken out now and then. All in the name of business, you know."

I looked at her. Sylvi was a durn sight more than cute, and "quite a little doll" was probably an appropriate description. And if I was reading her right, she was hinting that she wouldn't necessarily say no to a date. That wasn't what got my attention, but it might be a nice bonus for me.

"When could she start?"

"As soon as she knows what the pay is going to be."

I thought it over. Sylvi didn't know about the reward, so I could have whined about not having enough work to justify a secretary, but I already had an idea of just how valuable she might be. I didn't want to risk losing her or offending her by offering too little.

"I'm thinkin' somewhere around six hundred a week. Think she'd work for that?"

Her little brown eyes bugged out, and I laughed.

"Make it six fifty, and I'll talk her into it."

"Deal," I said, and held out a hand. She looked at it dumbly for a moment, then looked at my face.

"Oh, did you think I was talking about myself?"

I lost my smile. "You mean you weren't?" I asked in shock.

She held that innocent, puzzled kitten look for about three seconds, then burst out laughing. "Of course, it's me, you goofball! I had to yank your chain, though, and it was so funny!" She grabbed my hand, which was still hanging in the air, and shook it heartily.

"So," she said after she let go. "When's payday?"

The end

If you enjoyed this story, please leave a review. Your words really mean a lot.

Get a FREE *unpublished* Ned Fain story and be among the first to hear about Sam's new book releases and special deals when you join his email list here:

http://www.mix-booksonline.com/sam-abbott-insiders

See more adventures with tough, sometimes cynical private eye, Ned Fain:

http://www.mix-booksonline.com/category/sam-abbott

Sam Abbott

…is a pseudonym for a popular author of adventure and cozy mystery. Who is that, you ask? Well, that's another mystery.

Join Sam on his facebook page:
https://www.facebook.com/SamAbbottAuthor

If you enjoyed this book, you might like:

- Adventure/Mystery – **The Captain Finn Treasure Mysteries:**
    - The Mystery of the One-Armed Man
    - Black Bart is Dead
    - The Gold Doubloon Mystery
    - The Game's a Foot
- Adventure/Mystery – **The Agency Confidential series:**
    - Deceit
    - Cheat

www.ingramcontent.com/pod-product-compliance
Lightning Source LLC
Chambersburg PA
CBHW071212130626
46555CB00004B/1678